ALEXANDER AND HIS CURSED BOOK

SHIVANGI | PRATYUSHA GIRI | SAANVI SAHI

Alexander and his cursed book

Shivangi Saanvi Sahi Pratyusha Giri

Editor: Shivangi, Saanvi Sahi, Pratyusha Giri

Designer: Shivangi, Saanvi Sahi, Pratyusha Giri

Writer: Shivangi, Saanvi Sahi, Pratyusha Giri.

Introduction

The authors of this story are Shivangi, Saanvi Sahi and Pratyusha Giri. They are the students of Delhi Public School, Sail Township, Ranchi. They are currently studying together in class VI. They are very good friends. So, this is a horror story book which describes the life of Alexander which is completely changed after buying a cursed book. Alexander is a 11 year old boy who loves reading books. One day, he went to a book shop to buy a book. So he saw a horror book and made his mind to read the book. But he did not know that the horror book he is buying is cursed. The cursed book is a book which Alexander can never forget.

Contents

Characters

Alexander Higginson - An 11 year old boy

Thomas Higgins - The best friend of Alexander

Julia Higginson- Alexander's mother

William Higginson- Alexander's father

Sophie Higginson- Alexander's sister

Bob Higginson- Alexander's cousin

Emma Higgins- Thomas's mother

John Higgins- Thomas's father

Haster-A character in Alexander's book

David - Haster's friend

Chp-1

An introduction to Alexander

It was Sunday, and even it was 10 AM already, and Alexander, who woke up late in the morning, was still sleeping. His family was waiting at the dining table for him, but he was still sleeping. Now, his mother got really frustrated and she went to his room and strived a lot, but why will he wake up? Now at this moment she threw the whole jar of water on his face and finally, after so many efforts she made him awakened. After waking him up, his mother gave him some instructions to follow and finally after half an hour, he came to the dining table and had his breakfast. So the reason behind Alexander's late morning's, especially on Sunday's, was his dedication for reading books. He can't sleep without reading books. At least only a page, but he required a book in his hand to read. Yesterday he was reading a very interesting novel maybe, that's why he continued to read the book till 3 AM. Well, he loved all types of books- funny, science fiction, mysterious and even horror books.

Chp-2

The friendship

Today was the start of a new session at Alexander's school, and he was very excited. He went to his new class and he introduced himself to his teachers and even the teachers introduced themselves to the whole class. Alexander was sitting with a boy whose name was Thomas. He seemed to be really intelligent. His communication skills were also very good. So, I and Thomas became friends. First we talked a little bit and by the end of the school, these little conversations made us friends. Thomas was same as Alexander in studies. Alexander was also really good in studies and even his communication skills and vocabulary was very good as he read a lot of novels. Day by day, Thomas and Alexander became best friends. Thomas was also interested in reading novels so they even exchanged novels. But one thing was common for the horror book Alexander bought recently, that Thomas said that this book is really suspicious and I am really uncomfortable with it. Same thing was with Alexander. As Thomas was really uncomfortable, Alexander didn't exchange that book anymore. However, they became such good friends that they even didn't even think to eat without each other. Now one day, Thomas was absent. Alexander was thinking why is Thomas absent but how could he know the reason? So Alexander didn't eat his lunch as he thought that would be Thomas eating or not. The same thing was with Thomas, he was thinking that did

Alexander eat or not? Even if he ate his lunch in the school, I won't without him, and he had full faith in Alexander that Alexander wouldn't eat without him. The reason behind the absence of Thomas was that we was sick. So, Thomas was not eating without Alexander and Thomas's mother said that "Thomas please eat child, you are sick, if you will not eat food then how will you get energy"? like every mother cares. But Thomas's reply was that " I can't even think of eating without Alexander." Then there was no option left with Thomas's mother rather than taking him to Alexander's house. On the other hand, the same situation was with Alexander. Finally when Thomas reached Alexander's house, then they both ate their lunch together and even Alexander took a very good care of Thomas.

Chp-3

Shifting to a new house

So, it was 12 AM already, and it was raining along with thunderstorms. Alexander was reading the cursed book. So basically, he read that Haster shifted to a new house which was haunted. So after reading the book he slept, and the next day, when Alexander returned to his house, he got to know that they were shifting to a new house. Alexander was really sad to know that they are leaving their house in which they spent their precious time. But one thing was really making Alexander scared was that the thing which he read in the book came real. And in the book, Haster's mother didn't tell Haster why where they shifting. And even Alexander's mother didn't tell Alexander the reason for leaving their precious house. This was really scary. Alexander was really scared and he spent one whole night thinking this. Their 1st week was really good at the house but the start of the second week was horrible. Alexander was sleeping, then suddenly a woman woke him up and for sure it was not his mother as it was 3 AM at night. Then the woman just kept calling Alexander's name and at this moment, Alexander was just so scared that he screamed so loud that the next the neighbours where asking why someone was screaming at you home at late night. Well, Alexander's mother told them that Alexander saw a scary dream, that's it. But Alexander was telling that he really saw a woman but his mother did not believe him. The next night the same thing happened with Sophie. But his mother was not believing them. Now finally something horrible happened with his mother which made her believe Alexander and Sophie. At night 3 AM, she saw a woman. She was telling that " Leave the house, Leave the house his mother." If you don't then the result will not be good." If you don't leave the house I will kill your whole family." After saying this, she disappeared. The next day his mother and her family left the house and they started living in an another house, which was not haunted. But the same thing happened in the cursed book that Haster's family lived in an haunted house for a week and second week, some horrible things started happening and they left the house. The same situation was over here.

Chp-4

The sudden death

Saturday night Alexander read in the book that Haster's best friend died due to an unknown reason. Now after reading this Alexander was really scared, as the things which he was reading in the book was coming true. Now this thing Alexander couldn't imagine. He couldn't even think of eating without Thomas and living without him? No no no, this could never happen. But this was written in their destiny. On Sunday, Alexander woke up and he got the news that Thomas died due to an unknown reason. The death of Thomas was a mystery. But Alexander couldn't believe this and thought that her mother was lying.. But no, when he called Thomas's mother, he got to know that the news was true. Now Alexander didn't eat anything, he was just crying and roaming here and there in the memory of Thomas. He was thinking that Thomas left him but no, Thomas's spirit was always with Alexander. As in the cursed book, the spirit of Oliver was always with Haster. Now today was the funeral of Thomas, everybody was crying. Alexander was saying to Thomas's dead body that " Thomas, Thomas, you can't die. Wake up, wake up. You can't leave me alone. Take me too, but don't leave me alone. I can't live without you. But Thomas's spirit was always with his best friend Alexander.

Chp-5

The calls

So after the death of Thomas, Alexander was very depressed. He could not study properly, sleep properly or eat properly. Whatever he was doing he could not do that properly. Her mother was trying to distract him, but only he said was " Where are you, Thomas? Take me or come back, Take me or come back, Take me or come back. After a few days, he started reading books so that he can forget Thomas. So, it was raining heavily and Alexander was reading the book. In the book, he read that Haster used to get calls from his dead friend. So after reading this Alexander immediately looked at his telephone as he knew that Thomas is going to call him as whatever he was reading was coming true. So, after some time he got a call at exactly 12:00 AM. He just kept speaking that "Alexander I am your friend Thomas" 3 times and after that the phone automatically got cut off. This continued for a few days. Everyday he was getting calls. But he didn't tell his mother as he thought that she will never believe him.

Chp-6

Alexander gets a doll

One day, Alexander went out for a bicycle ride. He loved to ride bicycles. Riding bicycles was Alexander's hobby. He was enjoying a lot. He kept on riding his bicycle and slowly, he went to a scary forest by mistake. He was so excited that he didn't even know where is he going. The forest was very scary. Not a single person was there except Alexander. He was very scared and astonished to see such a kind of place. He parked his bicycle beside a tree and slowly walked forward. He looked around him. He was alone in such a big and scary forest. Scary sounds were coming from everywhere. He felt as if anyone is following him. He looked behind but no one was there. He walked to some distance and suddenly, he saw a doll lying on the ground. The doll was so scary. He took the doll in his hand and saw it carefully. After few minutes, an old lady came to Alexander and said " This doll is yours, my dear Alexander. It will give you a big surprise, your life will be changed after taking this doll. You will get something back that you lost. Alexander was very scared. After saying this, the old lady went on but Alexander was still thinking that what surprise will this doll give him. Why did the old lady said that and how did she know his name? Alexander was totally jumbled and he was not understanding anything. He was getting negative vibes. He felt as if anything strange is going to happen with him and his family. While he was thinking about this, it started raining. Alexander went to the place where he parked his bicycle. He took the doll with him and went home. But he was not knowing that the doll was having Thomas's spirit in it. After getting that doll, Alexander faced a lot of trouble. His life was totally changed.

Chp-7

The rare sounds

So, as the doll was having Thomas's spirit, it had to show some bizarre behaviour. Alexander usually doesn't like rain but today the rain attracted him and he went on the terrace to get wet. He was enjoying it but suddenly, some sounds were coming. He didn't know from where the sounds are coming. He could hear that someone is talking, screaming and laughing. He was feeling so scared that he immediately went to his room and after changing his wet clothes he just jumped on the bed and went inside the blanket. The blanket is the safest weapon from ghosts as per him. He could not sleep whole night as he was very scared. This same situation was in book. Alexander was now realising that something is really very wrong with the book. But he couldn't share it to anyone as he knew that nobody will ever believe him. The doll was making those sounds. In the book it was written that the doll made sounds. So now he was confirmed that something is wrong with the doll too.

Chp-8

The no reflection of the doll

The day was almost to get over and Alexander was getting bored. He thought what to do, he saw the doll and then he thought why not to play with it, then he took the doll in his hand and was moving around then he accidentally saw the reflection in the mirror, he was shocked his reflection was clear but the doll had no reflection. He shouted out loud and his mother arrived. She asked "What happened child, Why did you shout like this? Alexander replied "mom see on the mirror there is no reflection of this doll". Mom saw the mirror but all the reflections will clear. The dolls reflection was also clear. his mother said "Child are you gone crazy there is all the reflections very clearly visible on the mirror". his mother thought it must be some misunderstanding by Alexander. So, she made Alexander sit comfortably made him have some water and told him to relax. Then mom explained Alexander that there is nothing such, it's just his misunderstanding and made Alexander sleep but even his mother was shocked, she thought this really something wrong with this doll but she was not doing anything to do doll as she thought that Alexander will feel bad.

Chp-9

The talking of the doll

It was raining heavily outside. Alexander was going to read the book but then suddenly, a noise came. The noise was of a girl screaming. Alexander got really very scared after listening the voice. The voice was just like the voices in horror films. When he looked around, he found that nobody was there. Then he went to his mother's room to confirm whether everything was alright or not. When he went there, he saw that his parents were sleeping peacefully. Then he returned to his room and thought that " From where was the noise coming? It maybe our neighbours screaming." Then when again he was going to read the book, he heard that anybody was calling him. He turned back and again he saw no one. But then, he saw that the doll was moving. Then the doll said that " Alexander, I am back. I am inside this doll. Can you guess me?

I am Thomas." Alexander was shocked. He said that " You can't be Thomas. A doll can't be my best friend Thomas. But it was Thomas. The doll was repeating again and again that I am Thomas. Then Alexander suddenly fainted. The next morning, he told his mother that "Mom, Thomas's spirit came into my doll." his mother said that " Alexander, it must be your dream. How can Thomas's spirit come into a doll?" Alexander knew that his mother will not believe him. He tried to explain his mother but his mother did not believe Alexander. She made him calm and cooked his favourite breakfast. After eating his favourite breakfast, Alexander was happy but still he couldn't forget Thomas and whatever happened yesterday night.

Chp-10

Sophie's unusual behaviour

Days were passing and passing, Alexander with his family was sitting in his living room except Sophie. They all were thinking where is Sophie? They called her but there was no reply from her. They thought what's wrong? They went to her room to check where she is. They found that Sophie was sitting on the floor playing with Alexander's doll.his father asked what happened Sophie? We are calling you but you are not answering. But Sophie was as quiet as a non-living thing and continued playing. Sophie said don't disturb me, let me play with the doll and she was making ugly facial expressions. His mother said that "what happened child? Why are you behaving uneasy?" But unfortunately, no reply from Sophie came back. Then Alexander came. He questioned what happened mom and dad? Is everything going okay? Then suddenly, Sophie said to Alexander that "Hello my best friend! I am back. I am your forever friend Thomas!" Everyone was scared and shocked, especially Alexander. He thought Thomas spirit has came in Sophie. Shockingly, Sophie fell down feeling dizzy, and she closed her eyes, everyone was in tension. his mother brought a glass of water and sprinkled in Sophie's face. Then slowly she opened her eyes and asked "What happened to me Mom and dad? I cannot remember anything"! his mother said "Nothing happened my child, forget everything. Just think it was a nightmare." And then they made Sophie sleep but still Alexander was in tension thinking "Why was Sophie behaving like this? Did really Thomas spirit came in her?" But then after few days she was alright. But still Alexander can never forget this situation. At night, when Alexander was reading the book, the same thing happened with Haster's sister. Alexander was really scared.

Chp-11

An unknown boy

Alexander went to a park to freshen up his mood as his mother instructed him to do so. He was just sitting on the bench and seeing other people playing and thought " I wish Thomas would be there. I would also play like this with him." Now it was 7 PM already and Alexander was not home yet as he was lost in the memory of Thomas. Suddenly he realised that he need to go home otherwise his mother will be worried and scold him. As he started moving, near the gate he saw a boy just like Thomas. He was shocked. He asked him " What's your name? In which school do you study?" He replied " Leave these balderdash and listen to an important message from Thomas. I am sent by Thomas to warn you." Alexander could not believe his eyes but he had to believe. Now he said " I am also a friend of Thomas, but not such a good friend as you were. I am also dead. But the message from Thomas is that you should be very careful in doing each and everything. He even asked that "aren't you getting some negative vibes around you?" Alexander asked " Why should I be careful? But he disappeared. Now Alexander went running home as he was scared. He didn't tell his mom as he knew that she will not believe him.

Chp- 12

Bob's birthday party

It was Sunday, and finally, today was something more special, it was Bob's birthday who was Alexander's cousin. He with his family went to the venue and enjoyed a lot there. They ate Chinese, Indian, Italian, Thai and Mexican cuisine. Alexander played a lot there. All his relatives were there at the party so they talked, ate, played and did everything together. And while returning back, it was already 12:30 and if they took a longcut it would take 2 hours. So they decided to take the shortcut, but that shortcut route was considered haunted. But his mother and his father didn't believe in superstitious beliefs, ghosts, spirits, devil, monsters, and all these. So they decided to take this shortcut and even they didn't inform Alexander as they guessed he will be scared. So Alexander was clueless. Driving was going on and it was only 5 minutes of them driving on the shortcut, something unpredictable happened, Alexander could feel Thomas. He was getting negative vibes all around. Suddenly something near about impossible happens. Thomas appeared on the road but only Alexander was able to see him. Alexander shouted and told his parents but it was unbelievable for his parents. his father angrily said that "Alexander this is very well understood that you are depressed by Thomas's death but that doesn't mean you will speak anything! Just shut your mouth and sit silently." Suddenly it seemed that Thomas flew along the car and accidentally the car had an accident but shockingly, Alexander didn't even get a single scratch but his mother and his father had a fracture. A few weeks passed and his mom and dad finally recovered but they still think that Alexander is depressed. He is not behaving properly because of Thomas's death. That's the reason he could see Thomas and nothing else. But the dark truth is that really Thomas's sprit was present on the road and remember, he will always stay with him.

Chp-13

The camping nights

Alexander's school planned a 4 days camp in a nearby area. After hearing this good news, Alexander jumped in joy. As soon as he returned home, he told his mother about the camp rather than rushing to his room to read novels. Alexander prepared himself for the camp. He packed his bag for the camp. He was totally ready for the camp. So when Alexander went to sleep and started reading the novels, he read that Haster goes to a 4 days camp and his friends get disappeared day by day in the camp. Alexander was in fear thinking that everything he is reading is coming true, so will this also come true? But now Alexander calmed himself but still, he slept in fear. The next day they reached the camping spot and during the day, they did a lot of fun. At night, when everybody was in their camps, Alexander was walking to get the fresh air. When he came back, he did not read the book as he was scared that everything happing in the book was coming true. But he already read that Haster's friends disappeared day by day. So, the next morning when they woke up, they found that Alexander's one friend was missing. This continued for four nights. Everybody was thinking that "Why did it happen? How did it happen?" But no one could answer this. Alexander was really scared and he was in tension. But he could not tell anyone as he feared to tell. He also was thinking that " Why am I not telling?" But he didn't have an answer to this question.

Chapter-14

The reality

Alexander was sitting thinking about Thomas and the book. Suddenly, he could feel that someone was slapping him from here and there. He could not understand anything. Finally, he heard a voice calling him " Wake up, It's already the time for school. Wake up fast". When he woke up, he realised that everything was a dream. The death of Thomas, the doll, the cursed book, everything was just a dream. He was so happy that Thomas wasn't dead. He was still alive. He asked his mother that " Mom, where is Thomas?" His mother said " Have you gone crazy? Thomas must be at his home getting ready for school. What silly questions are you asking? Now stop these and get ready for school." When he went to school he was so happy to see Thomas. But Thomas couldn't understand why is Alexander so happy. When Alexander told him the full story, then Thomas understood everything. They both were happy in life

Contents

www.ingramcontent.com/pod-product-compliance
Lightning Source LLC
Chambersburg PA
CBHW031642170726
47990CB00018B/1631